Jennor

A Visit From

St. NICHOLAS

A FIREFLY BOOK

Published by Firefly Books Ltd., 1998
This paperback edition published, 1999

First Printing

Library of Congress Cataloging in Publication Data

Moore, Clement Clarke, 1779 – 1863.
A visit from St. Nicholas / story by Clement Clarke Moore ; illustrations by Kim Fernandes.
[32] p.; col. ill. : cm.

Known under title : The night before Christmas.
Summary: Unique Fimo three-dimensional illustrations accompany the classic verse.

ISBN 1-55209-429-4 (pbk.)
ISBN 1-55209-286-0 (bound)

1. Christmas—Juvenile poetry. 2. Santa Claus—Juvenile poetry. 3. Children's poetry, American.
I. Fernandes, Kim, ill. II. Title.

811/ .2 —dc21   1999   CIP

Published in the United States in 1999 by
Firefly Books (U.S.) Inc.
P.O. Box 1338, Ellicott Station
Buffalo, New York
14205

Published by arrangement with Doubleday Canada,
a division of Random House of Canada Ltd.

Designed by Kevin Connolly
Photography by Pat Lacroix Photography Ltd.
Printed and bound in Canada

TO DON

A Visit From
St. NICHOLAS

PICTURES BY KIM FERNANDES
STORY BY CLEMENT C. MOORE

FIREFLY BOOKS

'Twas the night before Christmas,

When all through the house

Not a creature was stirring,

Not even a mouse.

The stockings were hung
By the chimney with care,
In hopes that St. Nicholas
Soon would be there.

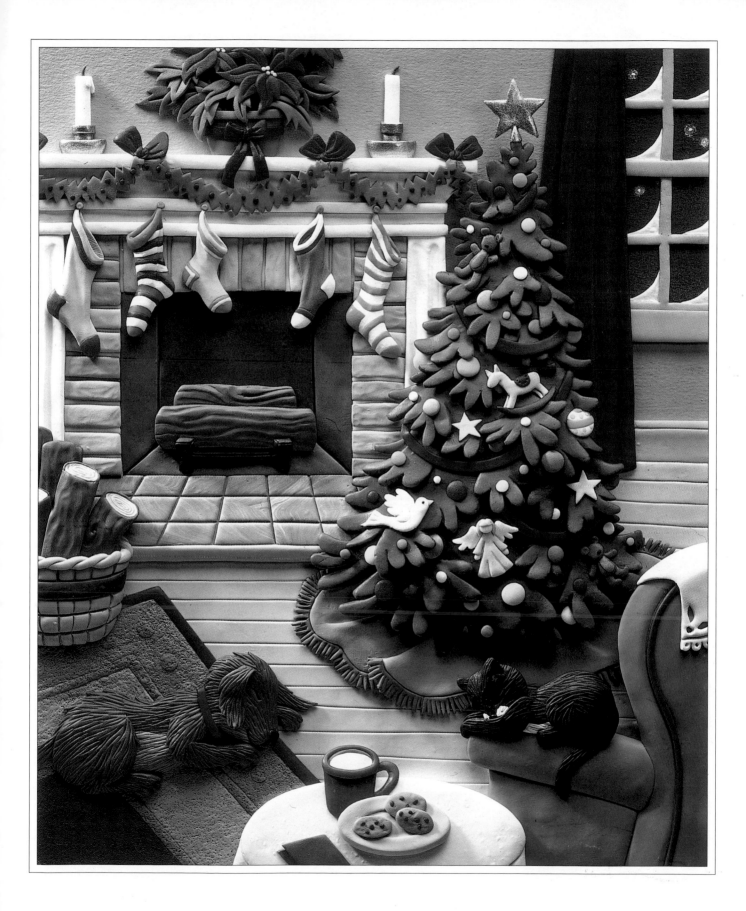

The children were nestled
All snug in their beds,
While visions of sugar plums
Danced in their heads.

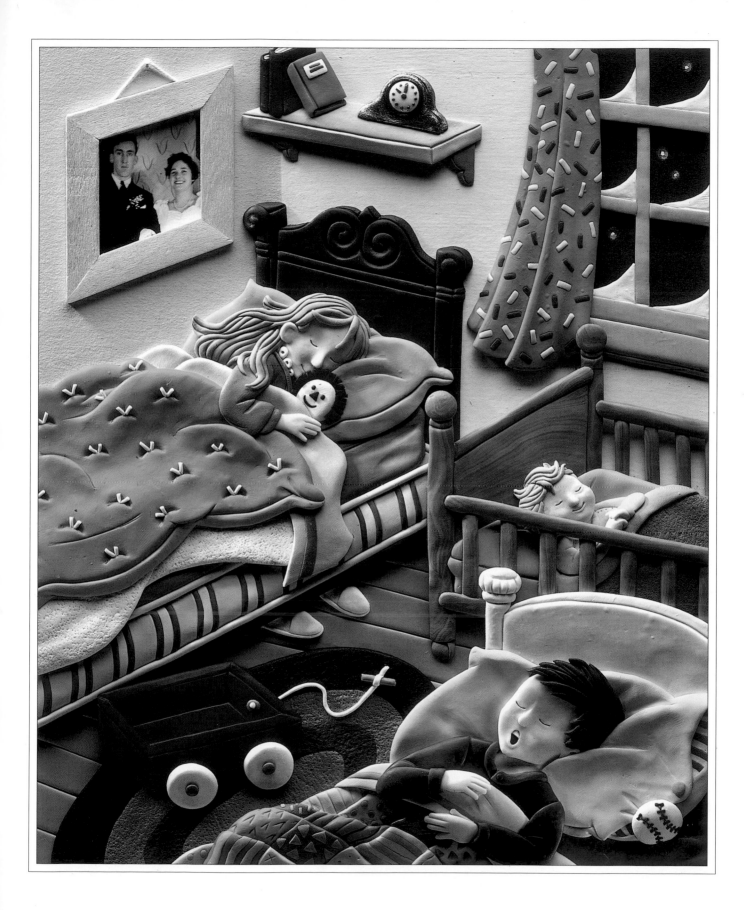

And Mamma in her kerchief,
And I in my cap,
Had just settled down
For a long winter's nap.

When out on the lawn
There arose such a clatter,
I sprang from my bed
To see what was the matter.

Away to the window
I flew like a flash,
Tore open the shutters,
And threw up the sash.

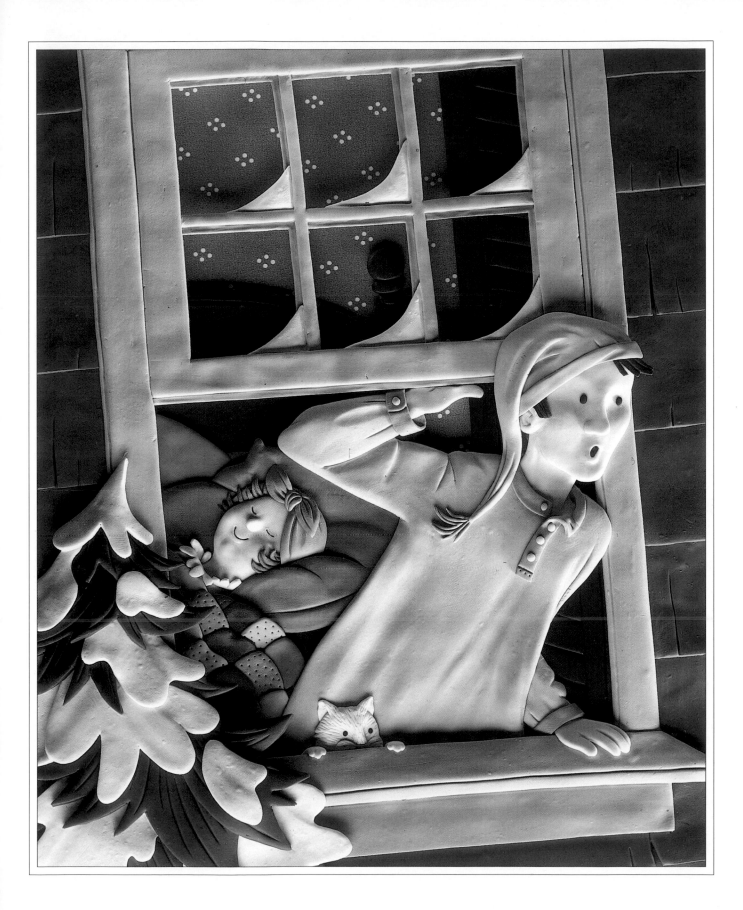

The moon on the breast
Of the new-fallen snow
Gave a luster of midday
To objects below,

When, what to my wondering
Eyes should appear,
But a miniature sleigh
And eight tiny reindeer,

With a little old driver,
So lively and quick,
I knew in a moment
It must be St. Nick.

More rapid than eagles
his coursers they came,
And he whistled, and shouted,
And called them by name:

"Now, Dasher! Now, Dancer!
Now, Prancer and Vixen!
On, Comet! On, Cupid!
On, Donder and Blitzen!

To the top of the porch,
To the top of the wall!
Now, dash away! Dash away!
Dash away all!"

As dry leaves that before
The wild hurricane fly,
When they meet with an obstacle,
Mount to the sky,

So up to the housetop
The coursers they flew
With a sleigh full of toys,
And St. Nicholas, too.

And then in a twinkling,
I heard on the roof
The prancing and pawing
Of each little hoof.

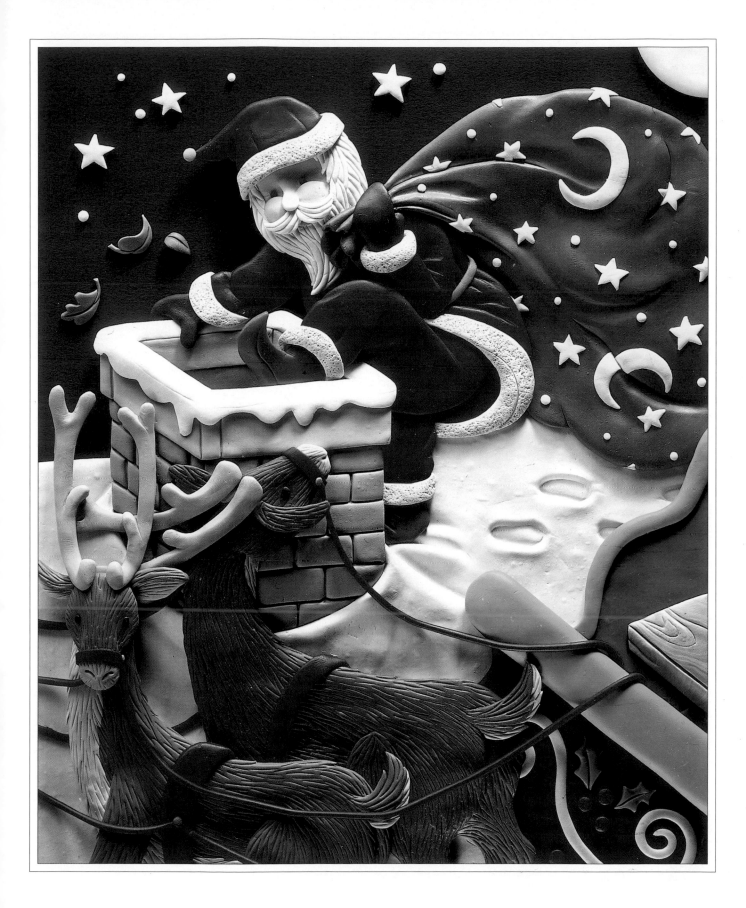

As I drew in my head,
And was turning around,
Down the chimney St. Nicholas
Came with a bound.

He was dressed all in fur,
From his head to his foot,
And his clothes were all tarnished
With ashes and soot.

A bundle of toys
He had flung on his back,
And he looked like a peddler
Just opening his pack.

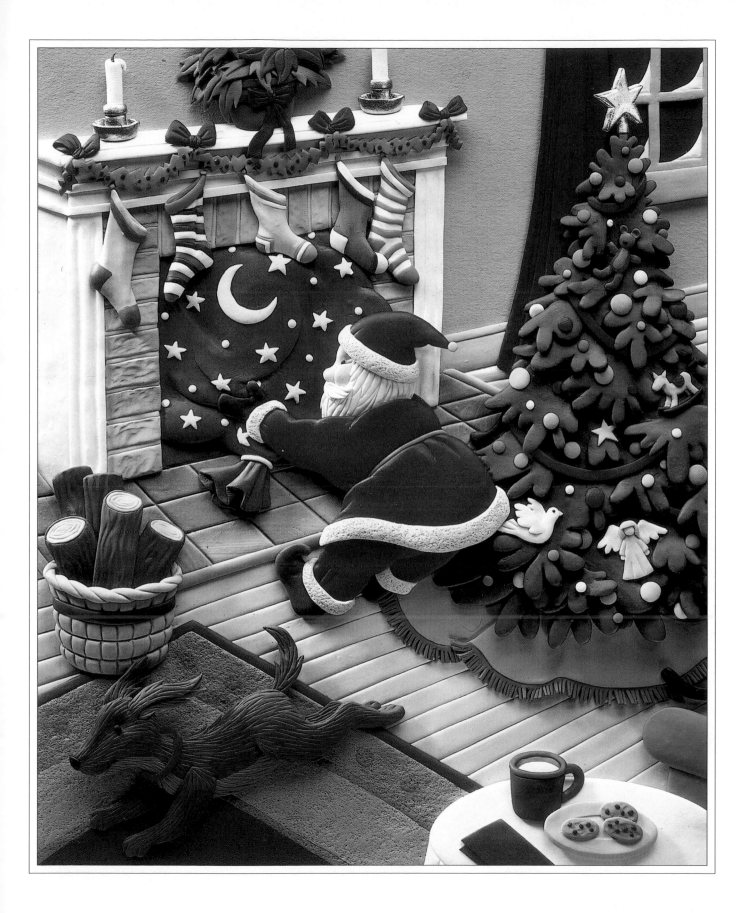

His eyes how they twinkled!
His dimples how merry!
His cheeks were like roses,
His nose like a cherry.

His droll little mouth
Was drawn up like a bow,
And the beard on his chin
Was as white as the snow.

The stump of a pipe
He held tight in his teeth,
And the smoke, it encircled
His head like a wreath.

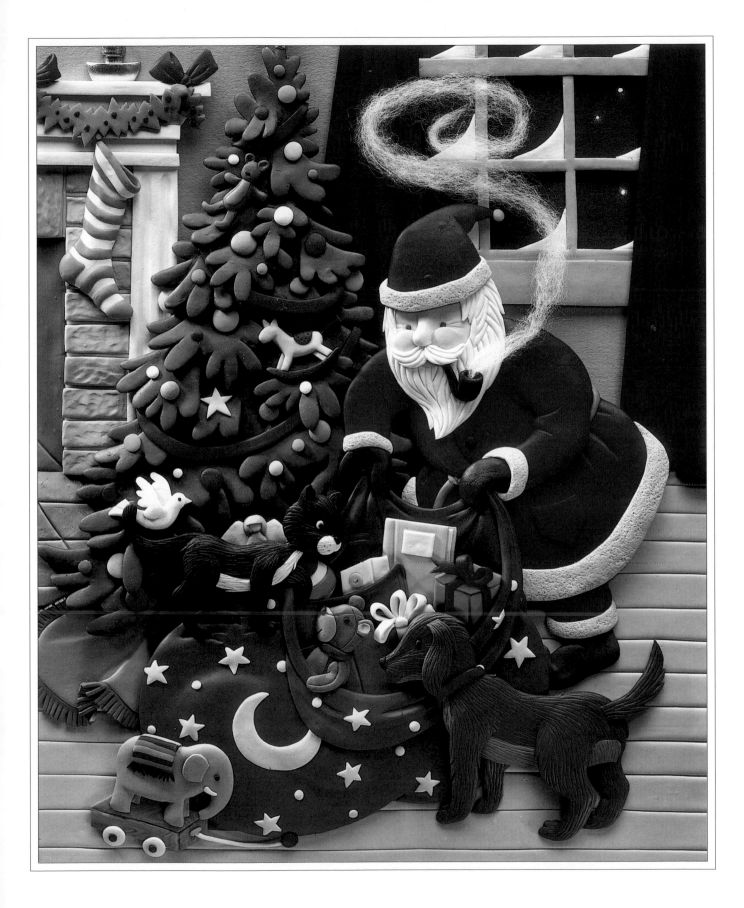

He had a broad face
And a little round belly
That shook, when he laughed,
Like a bowl full of jelly.

He was chubby and plump,
A right jolly old elf,
And I laughed when I saw him,
In spite of myself.

A wink of his eye
And a twist of his head,
Soon gave me to know
I had nothing to dread.

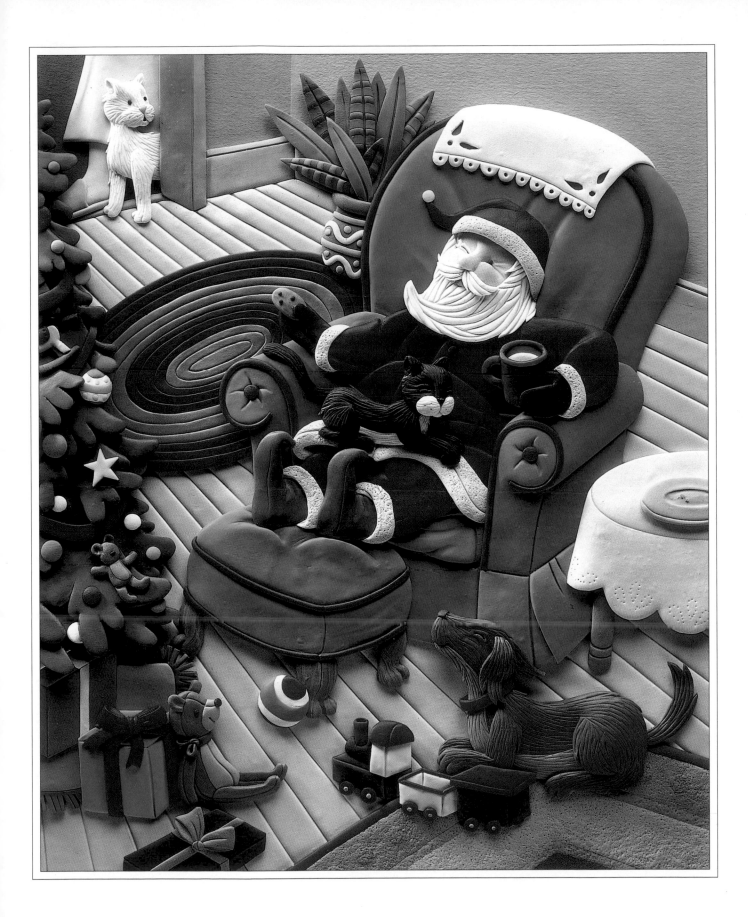

*H*e spoke not a word,

But went straight to his work,

And filled all the stockings;

Then turned with a jerk.

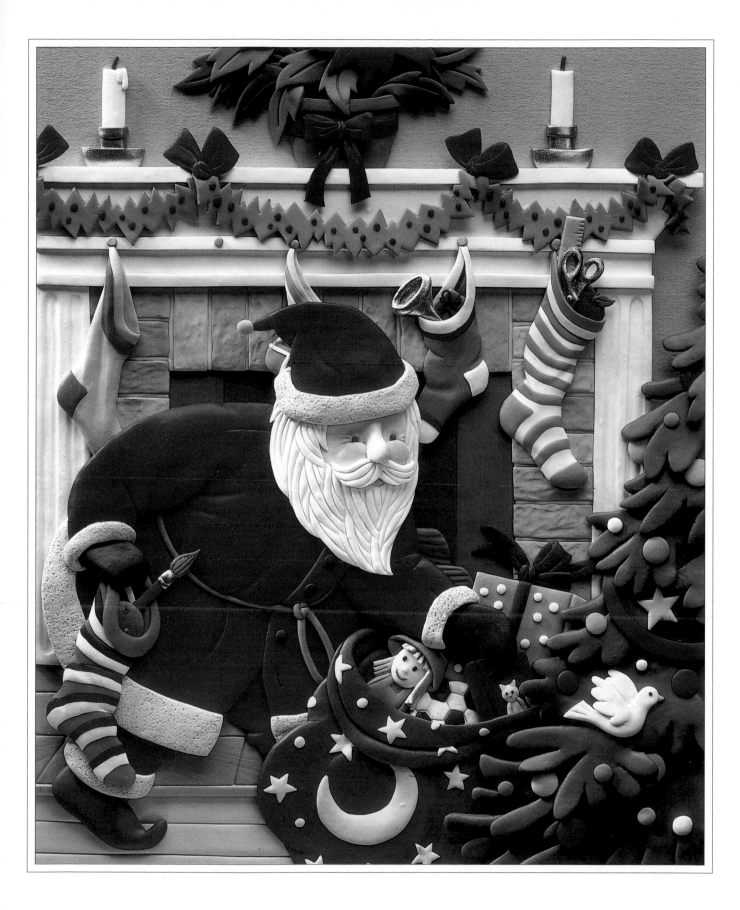

And laying his finger
Aside of his nose,
And giving a nod,
Up the chimney he rose.

He sprang to his sleigh,
To his team gave a whistle,
And away they all flew
Like the down of a thistle.

*B*ut I heard him exclaim
As he drove out of sight,
"Happy Christmas to all,
And to all a good night."

It is commonly believed that Clement C. Moore

wrote the original poem, "A Visit from St. Nicholas," in 1823.

The poem was first printed, anonymously, in

the *Troy Sentinel* of December 23, 1823. It was credited to

Moore in the *New York Book of Poetry*, 1837. Moore

himself acknowledged authorship in his book *Poems*, 1844.

Since then, millions of children—and adults—have

enjoyed this special verse.